RAINBOW magic

The Twilight Fairies

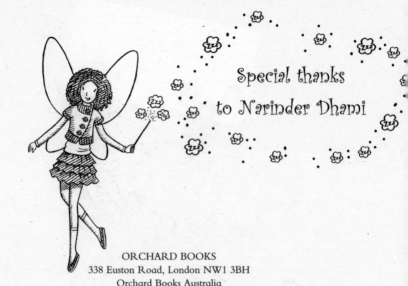

Special thanks
to Narinder Dhami

ORCHARD BOOKS
338 Euston Road, London NW1 3BH
Orchard Books Australia
Level 17/207 Kent Street, Sydney, NSW 2000
A Paperback Original

First published in 2010 by Orchard Books

HiT entertainment

A CIP catalogue record for this book is available
from the British Library.

ISBN 978 1 40830 912 4

7 9 10 8 6

Printed in Great Britain

The paper and board used in this paperback are natural recyclable
products made from wood grown in sustainable forests. The
manufacturing processes conform to the environmental regulations
of the country of origin.

Orchard Books is a division of Hachette Children's Books,
an Hachette UK company

www.hachette.co.uk

Sabrina

the Sweet Dreams Fairy

by Daisy Meadows

ORCHARD

The Fairyland Palace

Observatory

Fairy Homes

Ferry

CAMP STAR GAZE

Mirror Lake

The Twinkling Tree

Starry Glade

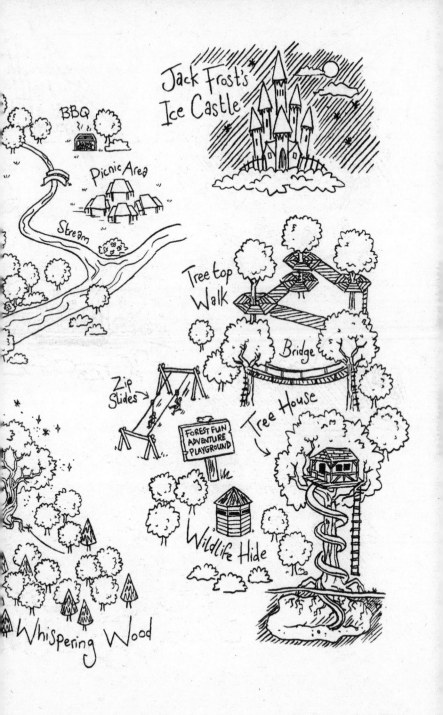

The Twilight Fairies' magical powers
Bring harmony to the night-time hours.
But now their magic belongs to me,
And I'll cause chaos, you shall see!

Sunset, moonlight and starlight too,
There'll be no more sweet dreams for you,
From evening dusk to morning light
I am the master of the night!

Contents

Nightmares!

"Oh, isn't it sad that this is our last night at Camp Stargaze, Kirsty?" Rachel sighed as she snuggled down inside her sleeping bag. She glanced up at the black velvet sky overhead, the tiny silvery stars glittering like diamonds. "Still, having an outdoor sleepover is a brilliant way to end the holiday!"

Kirsty nodded as she unzipped her own sleeping bag and climbed in. "It's been huge fun, hasn't it, Rachel?" she agreed. "I'm so glad we came!"

The girls and their parents were spending a week of the summer holidays at Camp Stargaze, which was so called because it was in a wonderful location to view the night sky. It was a warm, clear evening and all the children had brought their sleeping bags out onto the lawn beside the tents. They'd had juice and cookies, and Peter, the camp leader, had read them a bedtime story.

"OK, time to put your torches out now," Peter called. "Goodnight, everyone."

"I'd like to come back to Camp Stargaze again next year," said Lucas. He and Matt, two of Rachel and Kirsty's new friends, were lying on the lawn in their sleeping bags near the girls. "It's been the best holiday I've ever had!"

"I've learned a lot about the stars from Professor Hetty," Matt declared, switching off his torch. "And I'm going to carry on reading up about them when I get home, too. Goodnight, Rachel and Kirsty!"

"Goodnight," the girls called.

All the torches had been turned off now and the camp was in darkness except for the pale light of the moon. Gradually everything fell silent, although the girls could hear the occasional gentle hooting of an owl in the Whispering Wood nearby.

"No-one else knows that this has been an extra-magical holiday for us, Kirsty," Rachel whispered, smiling at her friend in the moonlight.

"Yes, we've had some amazing fairy adventures!" Kirsty whispered back.

When the girls had arrived at Camp Stargaze, their fairy friends had asked for their help once more. Rachel and Kirsty had been horrified to learn that Jack

Frost and his goblins had stolen seven
satin bags of magical dust
from the Twilight Fairies
while the fairies were at
their own outdoor party.

The Twilight Fairies
used their magic to make
sure that the hours between dusk and
dawn ran smoothly and were peaceful
and harmonious, just as they should be.
But with the magic bags in the hands
of Jack Frost and his goblins, all sorts
of strange things had been happening,
including a green sunset and the stars
moving around in the sky!

"I know we've found six of the bags,"
Rachel said, "But there's still one fairy
left to help – Sabrina the Sweet Dreams
Fairy."

Rachel, Kirsty and the Twilight Fairies had been determined to find the bags of magical dust after Jack Frost's icy magic had sent his goblins spinning away to the human world to hide the bags there. So far the girls and the fairies had managed to outwit the goblins time and time again and retrieve almost all of the bags.

"Let's hope we can find Sabrina's bag tomorrow before we go home," Kirsty said with a yawn. "Goodnight, Rachel."

"Goodnight, Kirsty," Rachel replied.

A few moments later, Kirsty heard her friend breathing deeply and knew she was asleep. Kirsty cuddled down in her sleeping bag, feeling comfortably warm and drowsy.

She gazed up at the sky, but suddenly she noticed that the light of the moon had vanished. For a moment Kirsty thought the moon had slipped behind a cloud, but then it reappeared for a second or two before disappearing again. It was almost like someone was flipping a switch and turning the moon on and off, Kirsty thought, puzzled.

Then she saw that the stars were moving. They were whizzing around the night sky, mixing up all of the constellations, and making Kirsty dizzy just to watch them.

Suddenly Kirsty heard a cold, icy chuckle very close by that sent a shiver down her spine.

"Ha ha ha! Those silly girls and their pesky fairy friends are no match for me this time!" Jack Frost gloated. "I have ALL the Twilight Fairies' magical bags, and now I am the master of the night-time hours!"

"Hurrah for Jack Frost!" the goblins cheered.

"No!" Kirsty gasped. "This can't be happening..."

Suddenly Kirsty jerked herself awake. She was all hot and flustered and tangled up in her sleeping bag.

"Oh, I was dreaming!" Kirsty sighed with relief. "I didn't even realise I'd fallen asleep. What a horrible nightmare!"

She glanced across at Rachel and was
surprised to see her friend sitting up,
yawning and pushing her hair out of
her eyes.

"Are you OK, Kirsty?" Rachel asked. "I
just had a terrible dream about Jack Frost
and the goblins!"

In the Starry Glade

"Oh, so did I!" Kirsty exclaimed, and quickly she told Rachel about her dream.

"My nightmare was that Jack Frost kidnapped all the Twilight Fairies and imprisoned them in his Ice Castle," Rachel said with a sigh. "It seemed so real."

"I think it might be because Sabrina the Sweet Dreams Fairy's bag of magic dust is missing," Kirsty pointed out. "Shall we go to the refreshments tent and make ourselves some hot chocolate? It might help us sleep."

"Great idea," Rachel agreed.

The girls slipped silently out of their sleeping bags, trying not to wake the others around them who seemed to be sound asleep. Then they tiptoed across the camp to the refreshments tent. Rachel fetched two mugs and Kirsty spooned some chocolate powder into them.

As the girls went over to the hot water urn, Lucas's mum stepped into the tent. She was carrying Lucas's younger sister, Lizzy, who was sobbing loudly.

"Oh, poor Lizzy!" Kirsty said. "What's wrong?"

"I'm not sure," Lucas's mum replied, giving Lizzy a comforting hug. "I think she must have had a nightmare. She woke up crying and talking about "greenies" – whatever they are."

Kirsty and Rachel glanced at each other as Lucas's mum went to get Lizzy some warm milk. "Greenies," Rachel repeated. "Do you think Lizzy was dreaming about goblins, Kirsty?"

"It sounds like it," Kirsty replied, frowning as she added hot water to their mugs. "There are a lot of bad dreams around tonight, aren't there, Rachel?"

"Like you said before, this must be something to do with Sabrina's missing bag!" Rachel said.

The girls took their mugs of hot chocolate and sat on a bench outside the refreshments tent under the stars.

"Look, Rachel," Kirsty said after taking her first sip of hot chocolate, "Here comes your dad."

Rachel glanced across the camp and saw her father. He'd just come out of the tent the Walkers and the Tates were sharing, and now he was wandering towards the girls. But as he got closer, Rachel and Kirsty could see that something was wrong. Rachel's dad didn't seem to have noticed the girls, even though he was staring straight at them, and he looked rather dazed and panicky.

"What's the matter with him?" Rachel asked, feeling worried. "Kirsty, do you think he's sleepwalking?"

Before Kirsty could reply, Mr Walker stopped abruptly. He blinked a few times and shook his head as if he was trying to clear it. Then he noticed Rachel and Kirsty staring at him.

"Oh, hello, girls," Mr Walker said, rubbing his eyes. Then he glanced down at his pyjamas, looking puzzled. "What

am I doing out here?" he asked.

"I think you were sleepwalking, Dad," Rachel told him. "Are you all right?"

"I'm fine," Rachel's dad reassured her, "But I was having a very strange nightmare. I dreamt I was surrounded by odd little green creatures with long noses and big feet! Then I heard cackles of icy laughter and I felt very cold." He shivered.

Rachel and Kirsty exchanged glances.

"Well, I'd better get back to bed," Mr Walker said with a yawn. "And so had you. We've got a long day ahead of us tomorrow. Goodnight, girls – I just hope I don't have any more nightmares!"

"Goodnight," Rachel and Kirsty chorused as Mr Walker went back to the tent. Then they turned to each other, eyes wide.

"Jack Frost and the goblins are getting into people's dreams!" Kirsty gasped. "What are we going to do, Rachel?"

"I don't know," Rachel sighed. "I suppose we ought to go back to our sleeping bags and wait for the magic to come to us. But I don't want to fall sleep again in case I have another goblin nightmare!"

The girls finished their hot chocolate, washed out the mugs and then tiptoed back across the camp. But before they reached their sleeping bags, Kirsty stopped dead, clutching Rachel's arm.

"Look, Rachel!" she whispered, "See that light in the Whispering Wood?"

Rachel peered through the darkness, and then she saw it.

A tiny, dazzling golden light was
floating through the wood, weaving its
way this way and that between the trees.

"Do you think it could be Sabrina?"
Rachel asked, excitement flooding
through her.

"Let's go and see!" said Kirsty.

Quietly the girls left the camp and
slipped into the Whispering Wood,
keeping their eyes fixed on the bright
light flitting around in the distance ahead
of them. It wandered here and there,
not seeming to be heading anywhere in
particular.

"I wonder where it's going?" said
Rachel.

Suddenly the light dipped down to the
ground out of sight.

"I think it's landed in the Starry Glade,"

Rachel guessed. "Come on, Kirsty!"

The Starry Glade was a little clearing in the Whispering Wood, covered with white, sweet-scented, star-shaped flowers. Rachel and Kirsty dashed into the clearing and saw that the light had settled on an emerald-green cushion of springy moss amongst the starry flowers.

"Kirsty, it IS Sabrina!" Rachel exclaimed in a low voice as they tiptoed closer.

Sabrina the Sweet Dreams Fairy was fast asleep on her bed of moss. She didn't even open her eyes as the girls bent over her.

"I wonder why Sabrina didn't come to find us?" Kirsty whispered.

Rachel frowned. "You know how my dad was sleepwalking?" she reminded Kirsty. "Well, I think Sabrina might have been sleep-flying! She was wandering all over the Whispering Wood, and she didn't seem to know where she was going."

Then Sabrina stirred a little. "Help!" she murmured in her sleep. "Help me!"

Rachel and Kirsty glanced anxiously at each other.

"Even Sabrina's having a bad dream," Kirsty said. "We'd better wake her up, Rachel!"

Ice Castle Mission

"Sabrina," Rachel called gently. "Wake up - you're having a nightmare!"

For a moment, Sabrina didn't move. Then slowly she opened her eyes and stared up at Rachel and Kirsty.

"Oh, girls, I'm so glad to see you!" Sabrina said shakily. She sat up, pushing her silky brown hair out of her eyes.

"I was dreaming that Jack Frost had captured me and imprisoned me in a cage of ice!"

"Lots of people are having nightmares about Jack Frost and the goblins, including me and Rachel," Kirsty told her.

"Jack Frost is using my bag of magic dust to give us all bad dreams!" Sabrina exclaimed, looking very upset. She fluttered off her cushion of moss, smoothing down her ruffled purple skirt. "I must get it back so that I can make sure everyone has good dreams again."

"Is the bag somewhere around here in the Whispering Wood?" Rachel asked eagerly.

Sabrina shook her head. "No, Jack Frost got so angry about the goblins losing the other six bags that he took the seventh bag back to his Ice Castle," she explained. "And now he's guarding it himself!"

Rachel and Kirsty glanced at each other in dismay.

"Girls, will you come to Fairyland with me and help me get my bag of magic dream dust back?" Sabrina went on. "You know that time will stand still here in the human world while you're away."

"Of course we'll come," said Kirsty. "Rachel and I don't want any more goblin nightmares either!"

Smiling, Sabrina lifted her wand and a puff of sparkling fairy dust whirled around the girls. Once again Rachel and Kirsty felt the familiar rush of excitement as they shrank down to fairy-size with their own glittering wings on their backs. Then, with another flick of Sabrina's wand, they zoomed off to Fairyland in a swirl of rainbow-coloured magic.

It was night-time in Fairyland when Sabrina and the girls arrived a moment or two later.

Sabrina swooped through an open
window in the Fairyland Palace and into
the throne room, Rachel and Kirsty right
behind her. To the girls' surprise, King
Oberon and Queen Titania were awake
and pacing up and down the room.
King Oberon wore a magnificent purple
dressing gown, while the queen was
dressed in a flowing white silk nightgown.
The other six Twilight Fairies were there
too, all looking rather anxious.

"Oh, girls, thank goodness you found Sabrina and woke her up!" Queen Titania exclaimed, rushing over to hug them. "We must get the bag of magical dream dust back. The king and I can't sleep because we're having the most dreadful nightmares about Jack Frost and the goblins!"

"Yes, I dreamt that Jack Frost stole my golden crown and wouldn't give it back," King Oberon said with a sigh.

"I had a horrible dream that Jack Frost became king of Fairyland, and the goblins were running around the palace gardens pulling the heads off the roses and paddling in the Seeing Pool!" the queen told the girls.

"And look out there." The king pointed out of the window at the toadstool houses surrounding the castle. Some of them were lit up by a bright firefly light, and as the girls and the fairies watched, more and more lights began to come on in the other houses.

"It looks like the whole of Fairyland is being woken up by bad dreams!" Sabrina said sadly. "But Rachel and Kirsty have agreed to come to Jack Frost's Ice Castle with me to try and get the bag back."

The king, the queen and the six Twilight Fairies looked greatly relieved.

"Once again you've come to our rescue, girls," said Queen Titania gratefully. "Thank you so much."

"And the other Twilight Fairies will do their best to make sure nothing else goes wrong here or in the human world before morning," the king added. "Take care, all of you."

Quickly Sabrina, Rachel and Kirsty fluttered out of the palace window again. Then they headed across Fairyland to Jack Frost's Ice Castle.

The girls had been to the Ice Castle
before, but as they fluttered through the
darkness towards it, it was
still a cold, scary sight.
The castle was
built of sheets of
ice with six tall
frosty towers, and
it glittered and
gleamed like marble
in the pale moonlight.

As Sabrina led the girls towards the
castle walls, they heard gruff goblin
voices. Immediately Sabrina put a finger
to her lips. There was a whole pack of
goblins standing on the battlements
talking to each other, and Sabrina,
Rachel and Kirsty floated down a little
lower so that they could listen.

"I'm tired," one of the goblins complained with an enormous yawn. "I want to go to bed."

"Jack Frost said we have to guard the castle against fairies and those meddling human girls!" another goblin reminded him.

Rachel and Kirsty glanced at each other. They could see goblin guards on all the entrances into the castle. How were they going to get past the goblins and slip inside?

Suddenly one of the goblin guards happened to glance upwards. He spotted Sabrina and the girls before they could duck out of sight and he gave a shriek of anger.

"Look!" he yelled. "Pesky fairies!"

Night
Monsters

All the goblins howled with rage and
rushed towards Sabrina and the girls.
Quickly the three friends rose up in the
air out of reach, and Sabrina began to
sing in a sweet, lilting voice:

When the sun has set at last,
When the sky is darkening fast,
When the moon is pale and light,

When the silvery stars are bright,
That's the time to rest your head
And climb into your cosy bed,
Sleep and dream the night away,
Tomorrow is another day!

As Sabrina sang her lullaby, the goblins stood staring up at her. Then they all began to yawn and rub their eyes. Rachel and Kirsty watched with a smile as the goblins began to sink down onto the ground, curling themselves up into balls as they fell fast asleep.

"Your magical lullaby has worked, Sabrina!" Rachel whispered as she and Kirsty flew down to join the fairy.

"Not quite," Sabrina said with a frown.
And she pointed at one of the goblins
who had stuck his fingers in his ears so
that he couldn't hear
the lullaby.

"I'm not
listening! I'm
not listening!"
he chanted
triumphantly,
running towards them.

"Quick, girls, into the castle!" Sabrina
cried.

The three friends swooped through the
nearest entrance and inside the Ice Castle.

"Stop!" the goblin shouted, giving chase.

"Where will Jack Frost be?" Rachel
asked as they whizzed down a corridor
of ice.

Sabrina frowned. "I don't know," she replied. "Let's try the Throne Room."

Sabrina, Rachel and Kirsty zoomed to the Throne Room and peeped inside, but Jack Frost's icy throne was empty. The goblin was still pursuing them so quickly they flew on.

"STOP!" the goblin yelled again, leaping forward to try and grab Sabrina. But luckily he missed.

"Maybe Jack Frost's in bed?" Kirsty suggested. "After all, it is night-time."

"But the Ice Castle is huge!" Rachel groaned as they turned another corner.

The goblin followed them, panting loudly. "His bedroom could be anywhere!"

Suddenly the goblin skidded to a halt on the icy floor. "I'm going to tell Jack Frost that you're here," he announced, "Then you'll be in big trouble!" And he turned and scurried up a winding staircase of ice in one of the tall towers.

"What luck!" Sabrina whispered with a wide grin. "The goblin's going to lead us straight to Jack Frost! After him, girls. But keep out of sight."

Rachel, Kirsty and Sabrina flew up the staircase after the goblin, keeping well back so that he couldn't see them.

They peeped around the curve of the stairs and saw the goblin come to a halt at the top of the tower outside a closed door.

"Look at the sign on the door," Sabrina whispered. "I think we've found Jack Frost!"

Rachel and Kirsty stared at the sign. It said: *Jack Frost's Private Chamber. Knock Before Entering.*

The goblin knocked on the door. There was a pause, and then Jack Frost stammered "C-c-come in!"

Kirsty was surprised.

"Why does Jack Frost sound so scared?" she murmured to Sabrina and Rachel.

The goblin went into the room, and
Sabrina and the girls flew in after him.
Through the dimness they could see
Jack Frost sitting up in bed, a frightened
look on his face. He wore white pyjamas
patterned with snowflakes and he was
clutching a blue teddy bear with icy,
spiky fur. A night-light was on the bedside
table next to him.

"I've come to tell you that there are
fairies in the castle—" the goblin began.

But Jack Frost had already spotted
Sabrina, Rachel and Kirsty, and the
frightened look vanished from his face.
With a roar of anger, he grabbed his
pillow and clutched it
tightly.

"I'm in charge of the
night-time now!" Jack
Frost declared firmly.
"And you'll never get
the last bag of magic
dust back!"

"Why aren't you
asleep?" Kirsty asked, still wondering why
Jack Frost had looked so frightened.

The goblin whirled round and glared
at her. "Jack Frost never sleeps at night,
didn't you know that?" the goblin
snapped. "He's scared of the—"

Jack Frost gave a yelp of rage and
hurled his teddy bear at the goblin. "Get
out!" he shouted.

The goblin scuttled out of the bedroom
as fast as he
could.

"What
are you so
scared of?"
Sabrina
asked Jack
Frost.

Jack Frost
frowned. "Night-time's very dangerous!"
he muttered. "There are Night Monsters
everywhere – and they'll get you if you're
stupid enough to go to sleep!"

"Where are the Night Monsters?" Kirsty
wanted to know.

"Everywhere!" Jack Frost replied with a shudder. "Under the bed. In the wardrobe. In the chest of drawers. Even in my slippers!" And he pointed down at a pair of icy, curly-toed slippers beside the bed.

"They keep me awake with bad dreams and if I've got to suffer—" Jack Frost scowled "— then I want to ruin night-time for everyone else, too!"

Sabrina glanced at Rachel and Kirsty.

"I don't believe it!" the fairy whispered. "Jack Frost is afraid of the dark!"

Sleepy Jack Frost!

"There are no such things as Night Monsters," Rachel explained to Jack Frost. "Look, we'll show you!"

Sabrina flew across the room and pointed her wand at the wardrobe. The doors swung open, showing Jack Frost's collection of icy outfits, but there was nothing else to be seen. Then Kirsty and Rachel flew over to the chest of drawers and together they pulled open the drawers one by one.

"See?" Kirsty said. "There's nothing there!"

"What about under the bed?" Jack Frost asked suspiciously.

Sabrina, Rachel and Kirsty linked hands and flew right under the bed from one side to the other.

"Nothing!" Sabrina said. "And there aren't any monsters in your slippers, either!"

But Jack Frost didn't look at all convinced. "Those Night Monsters are clever," he grumbled. "They can hide themselves away anywhere, and then pop up when I'm not expecting it!"

"There is one thing I can do to keep the Night Monsters away," Sabrina told him.

"What?" Jack Frost demanded eagerly.

"If you give me my bag of magical dream dust, I can sprinkle some around your bedroom and use my fairy magic to make sure you only have good dreams, never bad," Sabrina explained. "Then all the Twilight Fairies will have their bags back, and night-time everywhere will be peaceful and quiet and there'll be nothing to be scared of!

What do you say?"

Jack Frost hesitated, clutching his pillow.

"You could have wonderful dreams," Rachel chimed in. "You could dream that you're King of Fairyland."

"And that all the fairies are waiting on you hand and foot!" Kirsty added.

Jack Frost grinned. "Yes, that sounds like fun," he said. "Much better than lying awake listening for Night Monsters!"

Jack Frost reached inside the pillowcase
and pulled out the satin bag of magic
dream dust. Sabrina breathed a huge sigh
of relief as she flew over and took it from
him. Untying the drawstring, she took
a handful of dust and
scattered it around
the room. As
Rachel and Kirsty
watched, silvery
sparkles filled the
room, floating from
ceiling to floor like a
shower of snowflakes.

Looking sleepy now,
Jack Frost snuggled down under the
bedclothes. Sabrina, Rachel and Kirsty
picked up his teddy and tucked it in
beside him.

"Thank you," Jack Frost murmured dreamily. A few moments later he was sound asleep and snoring so contentedly that Rachel and

Kirsty couldn't help blowing him a goodnight kiss.

"We've done it, girls!" Sabrina whispered happily as Jack Frost snored on. "Now all the Twilight Fairies will be able to carry on with their night-time work. It's time to go back to the Fairyland Palace to celebrate. But first..."

Sabrina flew to an open window. Taking a pinch of shimmering silver dream dust from her bag, she blew it gently out onto the breeze. Rachel and Kirsty watched the dream dust shoot out into the night, swirling towards the Fairyland Palace in the distance.

"Now everyone in Fairyland will know I have my bag back," Sabrina said with a smile. "And there'll be no more bad dreams anywhere tonight! Thank you for all your help, girls. Now, let's go. I think there'll be a surprise waiting for us!"

Sweet
Dreams

As Sabrina, Kirsty and Rachel arrived
back at the palace, they heard the sound
of clapping and cheering. They floated
down into the palace gardens and saw
the king and queen and the other Twilight
Fairies waiting for them. They were
sitting on the palace lawns on soft duvets
and blankets with pillows to rest their
heads on.

"Welcome to our Twilight Party under the stars!" Queen Titania called to Sabrina and the girls as they fluttered down to join them. They landed on one of the soft duvets and made themselves comfortable.

"Well done!" King Oberon beamed at Sabrina, Kirsty, Rachel and the other Twilight Fairies. "If it wasn't for all of you, Jack Frost would still be master of the night."

"Poor Jack Frost," Sabrina sighed,
"He only stole the bags in the first place
because he's scared of the dark!"

"Really?" The queen looked amazed.
"So why did he play
all those other
tricks like moving
the stars around
and turning the
sunset green?"

"I think Jack
Frost decided he
might as well have some
fun causing chaos with our magic dust!"
Sabrina replied.

"But he won't do any mischief now
because he's fast asleep," Kirsty said
with a grin. "Sabrina gave him lots of
sweet dreams!"

Everyone began to talk and laugh about all the adventures they'd had, trying to get the bags of magical dust back from the goblins. Meanwhile, Ava the Sunset Fairy and Morgan the Midnight Fairy began handing round plates of star-shaped biscuits and mugs of hot chocolate with whipped cream. The girls joined in and had a wonderful time, but when Rachel spotted the fairies

beginning to yawn and Maisie the Moonbeam Fairy curling up on her duvet to go to sleep, she knew it was time for them to go home.

"I think we'd better go," Rachel told the king and queen. "Thank you so much for inviting us to the Twilight Party."

"You're our guests of honour," the king replied with a smile. "We couldn't have got all the bags back without your help."

"And we have a very special thank-you gift for you," the queen added. She handed Rachel a small satin midnight-blue pillow embroidered with a golden moon. Kirsty's was the same except that hers was patterned with silvery stars.

"The pillows are filled with a pinch of magical dust from each of the Twilight Fairies," the queen explained as the girls stared at the pillows with delight. "Now night-times will always be beautiful and peaceful for you both."

"Thank you," Rachel and Kirsty
chorused as the king and queen raised
their wands. Instantly, a shower of
colourful sparkles
swirled around
the girls as
they called
goodbye to
their fairy
friends.

Just a few
seconds later
the girls found
themselves back
to their human size at
the edge of the Whispering Wood in the
pale moonlight. Owls hooted softly as
Rachel and Kirsty tiptoed through Camp
Stargaze.

"It looks like everyone's sleeping soundly now," Kirsty whispered with satisfaction. She slipped into her sleeping bag and then laid her head down on the pillow the queen had given her. Rachel did the same.

"Sweet dreams, Kirsty!" Rachel said with a smile.

"Sweet dreams, Rachel!" Kirsty replied.

And in a moment or two, both girls were fast asleep, dreaming of their magical adventures with their friends the Twilight Fairies.

Now Kirsty and Rachel
must help...

Madison the Magic Show Fairy

Read on for a sneak peek...

Rachel Walker gazed excitedly out of the car window, as her mum parked. A short distance away she could see a helter-skelter, a spinning tea-cups ride, dodgems, and all sorts of sideshows and stalls. "This is going to be fun!" she said to her best friend, Kirsty Tate, who was sitting next to her in the back seat.

Kirsty grinned. "It looks great," she said, her eyes shining.

Kirsty had come to stay at Rachel's house for a whole week during the October half-term, and it was lovely

to be with Rachel again. The girls
always had the best time when they
were together… and the most exciting
fairy adventures, too! They had helped
the fairies in many different ways before,
although their parents and other friends
had no idea about their amazing secret.

"There," Mrs Walker said, switching
off the engine. She turned to smile at
the girls. "Do you want me to come in
with you?"

Rachel shook her head. "We'll be fine,
Mum," she said. "We're meeting Holly
near the helter-skelter in ten minutes,
so we'll go straight there."

"OK," said Mrs Walker. "I'll be back
here at three o'clock to pick you up.
Have a good time."

"We will," Kirsty said politely.

"Thanks, Mrs Walker. See you later."

The girls went through the park gates. There was a sign advertising the 'Tippington Variety Show' which was to be held at the end of the week, and Rachel pointed at it. "Mum's got us tickets for that as a treat," she said.

"A variety show… that's one with lots of different kinds of acts on, isn't it?" Kirsty asked.

Rachel nodded. "Yes," she said. "And they're holding auditions for the acts every day this week. Today they're auditioning for magicians. Lots of the schools around here have put forward performers, and the best one will appear in the Variety Show next Saturday.

My friend Holly's been picked from

our school to audition, so I said we'd cheer her on."

The girls walked through the fair together. Lots of people were enjoying the rides, or trying their luck on the stalls. They passed a hook-a-duck stall, a big rollercoaster and dodgems, and could smell sweet candyfloss, salty chips and fried onions. The auditions were taking place in a tent next to the helter-skelter.

"There's Holly," Rachel said, waving at her. "Wait till you see her magic tricks, Kirsty, she's really good. She's been practising non-stop lately."

Kirsty grinned. "And magic is something we know *all* about," she said. "I wonder if we'll meet any more fairies this holiday?"

"I hope so," Rachel said, lowering her voice as they approached Holly. "Oh, Kirsty, I really hope so...!"

Read Madison the Magic Show Fairy to find out what adventures are in store for Kirsty and Rachel!

Meet the
Twilight Fairies

Kirsty and Rachel must rescue the Twilight Fairies' magical bags from Jack Frost or nobody will ever enjoy a night's rest again!

www.rainbowmagicbooks.co.uk

RAINBOW magic

Meet the fairies, play games
and get sneak peeks at
the latest books!

www.rainbowmagicbooks.co.uk

There's fairy fun for everyone on
our wonderful website.
You'll find great activities, competitions, stories and
fairy profiles, and also a special newsletter.

Get 30% off all Rainbow Magic books at
www.rainbowmagicbooks.co.uk

Enter the code RAINBOW at the checkout.
Offer ends 31 December 2012.

Offer valid in United Kingdom and Republic of Ireland only.

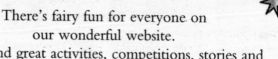

Win Rainbow Magic Goodies!

There are lots of Rainbow Magic fairies, and we want to know which one is your favourite! Send us a picture of her and tell us in thirty words why she is your favourite and why you like Rainbow Magic books. Each month we will put the entries into a draw and select one winner to receive a Rainbow Magic Sparkly T-shirt and Goody Bag!

Send your entry on a postcard to Rainbow Magic Competition, Orchard Books, 338 Euston Road, London NW1 3BH.
Australian readers should email: childrens.books@hachette.com.au
New Zealand readers should write to Rainbow Magic Competition, 4 Whetu Place, Mairangi Bay, Auckland NZ.
Don't forget to include your name and address.
Only one entry per child.

Good luck!

Meet the
Showtime Fairies

Collect them all to find out how Kirsty and
Rachel help their magical friends to save
the Tippington Variety Show!

www.rainbowmagicbooks.co.uk